Level
3

Superman:
Man of Steel

Written by Matt Jones

Contents

Meet Superman

Say hello to Superman! Superman is a strong and brave Super Hero. He protects people and fights Super-Villains. Superman is actually an alien from another planet called Krypton. The planet Earth is now Superman's home.

Superman's origins

Superman was born on the planet Krypton. Superman's people are called Kryptonians. Superman's Kryptonian parents, Jor-El and Lara Lor-Van, named him Kal-El. They sent their baby son to Earth in a spaceship to keep him safe.

Martha Kent and Jonathan Kent

Martha Kent and Jonathan Kent are farmers. They run a small farm just outside a town called Smallville. One day, they find Kal-El's spaceship in their field. The kind couple decide to adopt Kal-El. They name him Clark Kent.

Growing up

While growing up, Clark discovers that he has amazing superpowers. He goes to school in Smallville and makes friends with Lana Lang. At first, Clark doesn't tell Lana that he has superpowers. However, one day he must use his superpowers to save Lana from a tornado.

Superman's mission

Jonathan and Martha tell Clark to use his superpowers to help people. They don't want Clark to be selfish or mean.
Clark listens to his parents and uses his powers for good when he is older.
Clark becomes a Super Hero!

Superman's powers

Superman has many superpowers because he is a Kryptonian.

Flying
Superman can fly high into the air and can even fly in space.

Heat vision
Superman can release beams of very hot energy from his eyes.

Super-strength

Superman is super-strong. He can lift cars high into the air without getting tired.

X-ray vision

Superman can see through most things to help him understand how they work.

Superman's suit

Superman wears a special suit when he is fighting crime. His suit is blue, red, and yellow. It has an S-shield on it. Superman's suit is made of a special type of cloth. It is very hard to damage Superman's suit.

S-shield

Pants

Cape

Secret identity

Clark Kent wants to protect his family and friends so he keeps his identity as Superman a secret. No one else can know that Clark Kent is actually a Super Hero. While he is Clark Kent, Superman doesn't wear his special suit but does wear glasses.
Nobody notices he is the same person!

Krypto

Krypto is a superpowered dog from the planet Krypton. He is Superman's pet. Krypto is also the leader of the League of Super-Pets. This brave group of powerful pets fights crime.

Daily Planet

When Clark Kent is an adult, he moves to a city called Metropolis. He starts working as a reporter at a newspaper called the *Daily Planet*. Clark becomes good friends with Lois Lane and Jimmy Olsen.

Lois Lane

Lois Lane is a clever newspaper reporter. She has won many awards for her newspaper stories. Lois is brave and is not scared of criminals or Super-Villains. She later marries Clark Kent. They have a son together called Jon.

Jimmy Olsen

Jimmy Olsen is a photographer who works at the *Daily Planet*. He is also best friends with Clark Kent. He figures out that Clark Kent and Superman are the same person. Superman often has to rescue Jimmy from Super-Villains who have captured him.

Perry White

Perry White is an experienced newspaper reporter who is in charge of the *Daily Planet*. He must check all of the stories in the newspaper. Perry is a great teacher, and Clark and Lois have learnt a lot from him. Perry is godparent to their son, Jon Kent.

Superman's foes

Superman has many foes who want to try to defeat him. Some of them, like Doomsday, are aliens from other planets. Other villains, like Lex Luthor, are from Earth. Sometimes Superman's foes team up to face him in battle. Will they be able to defeat Superman?

Lex Luthor

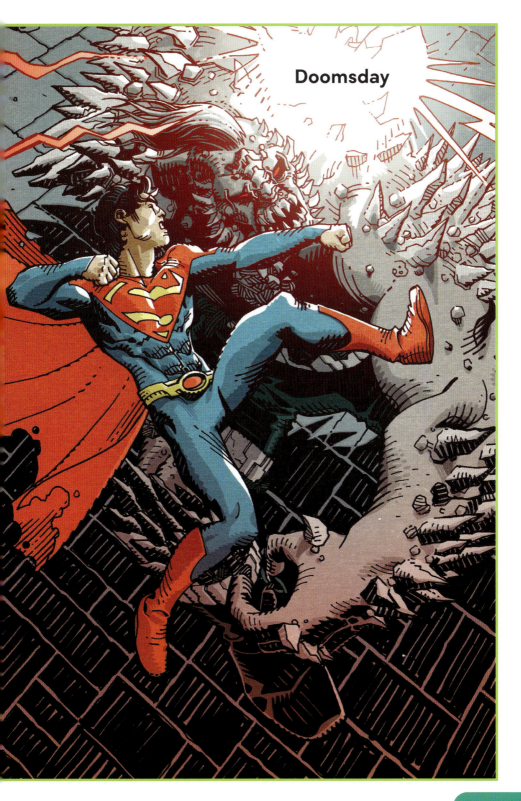

Doomsday

Cyborg Superman

Cyborg Superman used to be a human astronaut called Hank Henshaw. One day, his spaceship crashed and he had to transfer his brain into a computer to survive. Even though Superman did nothing wrong, Hank blames Superman for the crash. Hank has built himself a cyborg body. Hank names himself Cyborg Superman. He pretends to be Superman to try to ruin Superman's reputation. Will Superman be able to stop Cyborg Superman?

General Zod

General Zod is a Super-Villain from the planet Krypton. He was a criminal who was captured and kept in a special prison called the Phantom Zone. When Zod escapes his prison, Superman must try to stop him!

Lex Luthor

Lex Luther is a mean scientist and businessperson. He owns a company called LexCorp. Lex used to go to school with Clark Kent. When they are older, Lex learns that Clark is Superman. Lex is jealous of Superman's powers. Lex's employees help him plan ways to defeat Superman.

Mister Terrific

Superman can rely on his ally Mister Terrific. Mister Terrific's real name is Michael Holt, and he is a businessperson. He is very clever and has invented many pieces of technology. Mister Terrific uses his technology to fight Super-Villains. He is also the leader of a Super Hero team called the Terrifics.

Supergirl

Superman isn't the only Kryptonian Super Hero living on Earth. His cousin Kara Zor-El also crash-landed on Earth. She has the same superpowers as Clark. Kara grew up on Krypton so she is not used to living on Earth. However, she still decides to become a hero like Superman. Now known as Supergirl, Kara is always ready to help her cousin.

The Justice League

The Justice League is a team of powerful Super Heroes. The team works together to defeat the scariest Super-Villains and defend Earth. Superman is a member of the Justice League. His friends Batman, Wonder Woman, Green Lantern, and the Flash are also on the team.